TOWER HAMLETS PUBLIC LIBRARY

910 00

D1390529

POISON PAGES

BY MICHAEL DAHL
ILLUSTRATED BY MARTÍN BLANCO

Librarian Reviewer
Laurie K. Holland
Media Specialist

Reading Consultant
Elizabeth Stedem
Educator/Consultant

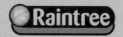

Raintree is an imprint of Capstone Global Library Limited, a
company incorporated in England and Wales having its registered
office at 7 Pilgrim Street, London, EC4V 6LB – Registered
company number: 6695582

"Raintree" is a registered trademark of Pearson Education
Limited, under licence to Capstone Global Library Limited

Text © Stone Arch Books, 2009
First published by Stone Arch Books in 2007
First published in hardback in the United Kingdom in 2009
First published in paperback in the United Kingdom in 2010
The moral rights of the proprietor have been asserted.

All righ   luced
in any f   ing it
in any i   ently
or incid   t the
writter   ance
with t   Act
1988   ght
Licen   lon
EC1   ht
owner'   sher.

LONDON BOROUGH TOWER HAMLETS	
910 000 00238078	
HJ	19-Nov-2010
	£4.99
THCUB	

Cover Graphic Designer: Brann Garvey
Interior Graphic Designer: Kay Fraser
Edited in the UK by Laura Knowles
Printed and bound in China by Leo Paper Products Ltd

ISBN 978-1406212709 (hardback)
13 12 11 10 09
10 9 8 7 6 5 4 3 2 1

ISBN 978-1406212846 (paperback)
14 13 12 11 10
10 9 8 7 6 5 4 3 2

British Library Cataloguing in Publication Data
Dahl, Michael.
Poison pages. -- (Library of doom)
813.5'4-dc22
A full catalogue record for this book is available
from the British Library.

TABLE OF CONTENTS

The Library of Doom is the world's largest
collection of strange and dangerous books.
The Librarian's duty is to keep the books
from falling into the hands of those who
would use them for evil purposes.

74

CHAPTER 1

THE EMPTY SEAT

The city is grey and cold. Rain falls from an angry sky.

A young girl holds an umbrella and waits for the bus to take her home.

The bus arrives full of sad,
sleepy passengers.

The girl finds a place to sit, but
there is a small, square shadow
on the seat.

"Someone forgot their book,"
the girl says to herself.

She picks up the shadowy book
and looks at the cover. Weird letters
spell out The Lost Readers.

When she turns a page, the girl sees a picture of a grey girl waiting for a bus. The grey girl climbs onto a grey bus and finds a seat.

On the next page is another picture. It shows the grey girl's seat, but this time the girl is gone.

Suddenly, on the real bus, the real girl is gone, too.

Only the **shadowy** book is left behind.

CHAPTER 2

THE ENDLESS FLOOR

The girl is no longer on the bus. She is outside. She is standing on a wide, flat floor. The floor is endless.

The endless floor is covered with black shapes.

She bends down and sees that the shapes are painted on the floor.

"Letters," says the girl.

"I am inside the book," she says to herself.

In the distance, the girl sees another shape. It is a man walking towards her.

The girl is frightened. She turns to walk away.

"Stop!" shouts the man. "Take one more step, and it will be your last!"

CHAPTER 3

THE LOST READERS

"Who are you?" asks the girl.

"I am the Librarian," says the man. "You have been taken by the book. Along with the others."

"Others?" says the girl.

The girl looks and now she can see other shapes.

Men, women, and children crowd around the **edges** of the endless floor.

"Who are they?" asks the girl.

"The lost readers," says the Librarian. "We are all inside the pages of the book."

The girl takes a step forward.

"I told you not to move," said the Librarian. "Do you want to end up like that?"

He points to a **figure** lying near them.

CHAPTER 4

A POISON PATH

The girl looks down. She was about to step on one of the <u>letters</u>.

"The letters are made of poison ink," says the Librarian.

"If you touch the poison, you will become part of the book forever."

"I've never heard of a poison book," says the girl.

"It is not an ordinary book," he says. "It comes from the Library of Doom."

"Follow me," he says. "Put your feet where I put mine."

Carefully, they walk across the `endless` floor.

"Let go!" the girl shouts.

One of the figures has grabbed
her foot.

CHAPTER 5

TRAPPED ON THE PAGE

"Why?" gasps the figure. "Why?"

The Librarian bends down and frees the girl's foot from the figure's grasp.

"He was poisoned by a question mark and cannot stop asking questions," says the Librarian.

The girl looks into the distance. She can see a faraway shape. It looks like a giant wave.

"The page is turning," says the Librarian.

The girl and the man race across the **vast floor**. $\longrightarrow$

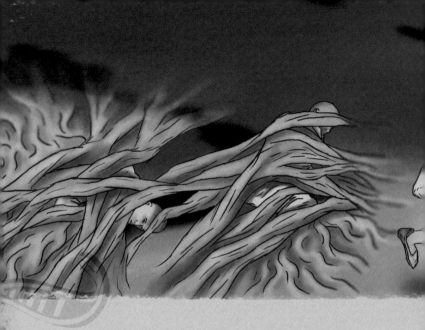

"Who are they?" asks the girl.

She sees some people tightly
wrapped with strips of paper.

They cannot move their arms or
legs. She hears them **moan**.

"Those are the library bound,"
says the Librarian.

"We cannot stop to help them."

The girl looks behind her. The
giant wave is **growing** closer.

CHAPTER 6

OVER THE EDGE

The Librarian suddenly stops.

They are standing at the edge of the page.

Below them is a great darkness.

"You must jump," says the Librarian.

"But there's nothing there," the girl says.

"Trust me," says the Librarian.

The **giant** page is getting closer and closer.

"All right," says the girl.

She closes her eyes. She takes a
deep breath and jumps.

The **wind** rushes past her body.

Bump!

The girl opens her eyes. She is back on the bus.

She looks down at the book and sees a picture of the Librarian.

Why didn't he jump? the girl wonders.

At the bottom of the page she sees the words: There are more lost readers who **need my help**.

∾◦ **THE END** ◦∾

A PAGE FROM THE LIBRARY OF DOOM

LETTERS

Cambodia has the world's largest alphabet with 74 letters.

The world's shortest alphabet is used in the Solomon Islands of the South Pacific. It has only 11 letters.

Hawaiian is the next shortest with only 12 letters:

A E I O U H
K L M N P W

The most common letter in English is E.

W is the only letter in English that has more than one syllable.

In almost every language on Earth, the word for "mother" begins with the letter M.

ABOUT THE AUTHOR

Michael Dahl is the author of more than 100 books for children and young adults. He has twice won the AEP Distinguished Achievement Award for his non-fiction. His Finnegan Zwake mystery series was chosen by the Agatha Awards to be among the five best mystery books for children in 2002 and 2003. He collects books on poison and graveyards, and lives in a haunted house in Minneapolis, USA.

ABOUT THE ILLUSTRATOR

Martín Blanco was born in Argentina and studied drawing and painting at the Fine Arts University of Buenos Aires. He is currently a freelance illustrator and lives in Barcelona, Spain where he is working on films and comic books. Blanco loves to read, especially thrillers and horror. He also enjoys playing football, the Barcelona football team, and playing the drums with his friends.

GLOSSARY

bound (BOWND) – trapped, tied up

grasp (GRASP) – to grab something firmly

seep (SEEP) – to flow slowly

vast (VAST) – very large

weird (WEERD) – strange

DISCUSSION QUESTIONS

1. At the end of the story, the girl is back on the bus. What do you think she should do with the book she found there? Why?

2. The Librarian is staying inside the book to help more lost readers. Do you think he will be able to rescue any more of them? Why or why not?

3. Sometimes people say they can "get lost" in a book. What do you think they mean by that?

WRITING PROMPTS

1. Imagine that you are trapped inside a book. It can be a real book that you have read, a comic book, or a book that you just made up. Write a story and describe what adventures you have. Are you able to escape?

2. What happens to the Librarian after the girl leaves? Who does he rescue next? What happens to him when the page turns? Write the next chapter in the Librarian's story.

MORE BOOKS TO READ

This story may be over, but there are many more dangerous adventures in store for the Librarian. Will the Librarian be able to escape the cave of the deadly giant bookworms? Will he defeat the rampaging Word Eater in time to save the world? You can only find out by reading the other books from the Library of Doom...